JESUS ONLY

SHELLEY FRINKLEY

ISBN 979-8-67566-945-5 (Paperback)

John Mark was a drunk and spent most of his time sitting in the neighborhood bar. John was once in the army and fought in the Korean War. John also jumped out of airplanes during the Korea War. But after the war and a failed marriage, he lost all self-respect for himself. His whole life changed. John was once a very respectable man, and now he just sits in the bar all night, drinking his problems away.

But that night in 1956, John came out of the bar sometime after midnight just like every night to walk home. He would walk down the alley to his parents' house. However, that night there was a man standing against the light pole outside the bar, waiting for John to come out. This wasn't an ordinary man. John thought he was just a man, and he didn't really look at him standing outside the bar.

John began to walk home. He heard someone walking behind him, but he didn't look back. He just kept on walking home, but the sound got closer and closer. The man called him by his name, "John, John, John."

He stopped and turned around. "Who are you?"

It was the man outside the bar. But he looked different, he had chains all over his body, and he was surrounded by light. John knew this was not an ordinary man.

The chain man said to John, "You have to change your life."

John started to run home down the alley. He was screaming and running, falling down as he was trying to get to his house. The chain man was still behind him, talking to him all the way home. John was screaming, "No, no, no, no."

And the chain man was still talking to him as he was running. The chain man said, "John, you have to live for Jesus. You have to change your life. John, you have to live for Jesus, or your life is over tonight."

The chain man was still behind him.

John was screaming and crying and running, trying to get to his house. John reached the front porch of the house, "Mama, Mama, Mama, open the door, open door!"

The chain man was on the porch still talking to him.

John was screaming, "Mama, open the door! There's a man after me!"

His mother came to the door. John told his mother he had to get saved tonight, "Mama, can you see the chain man?"

His mother said, "What man? Boy, you've been drinking too much."

"Mama, he is there, and he is in chains."

John's mother couldn't see the chain man, but she knew it was true.

John was saying over and over again, "I have to change my life, and I have to get baptized and filled with the Holy Ghost tonight." John told his mother that a chain man chased him all the way home that he was a message from God. John said, "If I don't change my life, I was going to die tonight. That is what the chain man said. I have to live for Jesus. No more drinking and smoking. I have to live a clean life. I want to live, Mama."

John's mother began to cry out, "O Lord, O Lord, I'll call my minister right now at his home."

The reverend said, "Bring him to the church tonight."

That night in 1956, John was baptized and filled with the Holy Ghost. John came out of water, speaking in tongues, saying, "Jesus, Jesus, Jesus, Jesus," over and over again. "I have to live for Jesus. The angel of death sent by God told me to live for Jesus, and I have fifteen years to do it. The angel of death was standing outside the bar that night, but God gave me a second chance to turn my life around. Tonight, Jesus has changed me. I've got a new walk, new talk, and it feels so good inside my soul. Jesus said, 'Tell everyone you meet about Jesus Christ.' However, from that night on, I'm living for Jesus, and I have left that old life behind. And I'll never looked back because if I do, I would lose my soul. Thank you, Hallelujah. Psalm, O God, forgive me, O Lord, for I have sin, O Lord, clean me, wash me, O Lord, that I may be whiter then snow. Have mercy upon me, O Lord. Lord, I acknowledge my sins against thee, thee only, have I sinned and done this evil in thee sight, O God. O Lord, make me to know wisdom. Lord Jesus create in me a clean heart, O God, and renew a right spirit with in me, Jesus. O Lord, open thou my lips and my mouth, and I shall show forth thy praise. All the days of my life, O Lord Jesus."

And every day of John's life was to talk to someone about the Lord, or he would preach at a church. Also John would visit people in hospitals and nursing homes. He wanted everyone to know about Jesus and how much he loves you. John received the gift of preaching, and he would go from church to church, preaching the Gospel of Jesus Christ.

Rev. John Mark would say to the people he met, "All you have to do is ask Jesus, and Jesus will help you." Rev. John Mark would tell strangers he met to go to church on Sunday. Rev. John Mark lived for Jesus only. He would visit different churches. And Rev. John Mark would tell people he met about how Jesus saved him from a life of sin. Rev. John Mark would pray for people he met if they wanted him to. Rev. John Mark would tell the people he met to read their Bibles every day. Rev. John Mark would smile, and his love for Jesus was in his eyes, and you could see it and feel it when he talks to you. And you would hear it in his voice how much he loved Jesus Christ that he was a man of God.

Rev. John Mark had to pray every day to get closer to his Lord Jesus by which God would talk to him and show him different things. He wanted him to do, to help people he met. Rev. John Mark wanted to tell the whole world about Jesus only. Rev. John Mark visited churches in Ohio, Chicago, Cleveland.

Every day was a day to serve Jesus Christ. Rev. John Mark would not leave the house without his Bible. Rev. John Mark would wake up with the Lord in his mind, and go to bed with the Lord in his mind. Rev. John Mark loved Jesus with his whole heart, and gave his soul to the Lord Jesus.

Everywhere Rev. John Mark went, Jesus was with him in spirit. Jesus sent John a wife to love him, and he married Mary.

Rev. John Mark and Mary lived as one. Rev. John Mark worked for Ford Motor Co., but he always had time for Jesus. Rev. John Mark had five thousand bottoms made, which said *Jesus Only*. And Rev. John Mark would give everyone he met a pin to wear. "Jesus wants you to live a good life. Jesus wants you to come to him with your problems."

Psalm 69 says, "Save me, O God, for the waters are come in unto my soul. I sink in deep mire, where there is no standing. I am weary of my crying. My throat is dried, my eyes fail while I wait for my God."

Rev. John Mark received calls from other churches, asking him to come and preach at their church. Rev. John Mark would visit as many churches to talk about Jesus. There was so many churches who wanted him to come. They would offer him money to come to their church. Rev. John Mark was a messenger of God. Rev. John Mark had to work for God every day of his life. Rev. John Mark would preach about different prophets like Jeremiah, Moses, also young Daniel.

Rev. John Mark would travel, preaching the Gospel of Jesus Christ, and he would tell the church members, "Help, Lord. Send peace. And Lord, keep me safe from evil. I trust in you, O Lord Jesus, goodness and mercy shall follow you all the days of my life, and I will dwell in the house of the Lord forever. King David trusts in Jesus."

The whole church was on their feet with their arms up.

"Call him, call him, Jesus, Jesus, over and over again. Amen. Amen."

Rev. John Mark began singing with the church members. Rev. John Mark told the church members to "pick up the cup of life, and drink of this cup that Jesus gives, and you shall never thirst. Jesus also said, 'Whosoever eateth my flesh, and drink my blood, has eternal life. Amen. Thank you, Jesus."

Rev. John Mark continued talking about Jesus, "And this, the will of him that send me, that everyone which seethe the son and believed in Jesus only." Rev. John Mark would tell the members of the church to trust in the Lord, for the Lord Jesus will help you. "If you ask any thing in my name, I will do it." King David, Psalm 40 says, "I waited patiently for the Lord, and he inclined unto me and heard my cry. He brought me up also out of a horrible pit, out of the miry clay, and set my feet upon a rock, and established my goings. And he put a new song in my heart, and I shall trust in the Lord."

Rev. John Mark believed in the word of God, and he lived by the rules of God. Rev. John Mark traveled to Ohio to preach. Rev. John Mark said, "Tonight, I want you to put on the whole armor of God that you may be able to stand against the devil." Rev. John Mark said," Keep your mind on God because he will help you see wiles of the devil, keep your mind on the Lord at all times. For we wrestle not against flesh and blood but against principal, against power, against the rulers of the darkness in high places. Amen. Amen."

The saints of God were on their feet with arms stretched out to God. "Sometimes you can't see the evil, my God. But evil is there standing in front of you. Amen. But God can help you see the devil coming at you. Thank you, Jesus. Thank you, Jesus. Jesus, let me see the devil coming at me, O Lord. O Lord."

At that point, the whole church was on their feet speaking in tongues. "O Lord Jesus. Amen. Jesus, Jesus."

Rev. John Mark was saying to the whole church, "Have the breastplate of righteousness, and your feet shod with the preparation of the gospel of peace. Above all, taking the shield of faith where with you shall be able to quench all fiery darts of the wicked, and take the helmet of salvation, and the sword of the spirits of God, which is the word of God."

The whole church was in the spirit of God.

Rev. John Mark said, "Hold on to name's sake. Yeah, though I walk through the valley of the shadow of death, I will fear no evil, for thou art with me, thou rod, and thou staff, they comfort me. Thou prepare a table before me in the presence of my enemies, thou anointest my head with oil, my cup runneth over. Surely goodness and mercy shall follow me all the days of my life, and I will dwell in the house of the Lord forever."

Rev. John Mark praised God at all times for goodness and mercy. Rev. John Mark traveled from church to church, preaching the Gospel of Jesus Christ. Rev. John Mark said, "Nothing is impossible for God and believe that all things are possible with God. Saints of God believe today as servants of God. Let the whole church say amen, amen. Jesus came so you may have life more abundantly.

"In John 10:10, the thief cometh but to steal, and to kill, and to destroy. I come that they might have life and that they might have it more abundantly. Hallelujah, thank you, Jesus. Thank you, Jesus.

"Jesus said that, and it is writings in the Bible, 'I am the way, the truth, and the life. No man cometh unto the Father but by me.' Let the whole church give our Lord his praise, stand up, saints of God. Give our Lord his praise. Thank you, thank you, thank you, Jesus.

"Lord Jesus came into the world to save us from our sins. Jesus said, 'That whosoever believeth in him should not perish but have eternal life.' Amen. Saints of God, put your trust in God. Jesus said, 'Ask anything in my name, and I'll do it.' Amen. Let the church say amen, amen. Jesus said, 'Peace, I leave with you, my peace, I give unto you, not as the world giveth, I give unto you.' Amen, amen. Jesus said, 'Let not heart be troubled, neither let it be afraid.'"

Rev. John Mark said, "Do not be afraid, come to God today, give your life to God. Amen. Come, come, let me baptize you. Amen. Come to God, come, give up that old life. Hallelujah, thank you, Jesus. Amen. The Gospel of Jesus Christ. Amen. Thank you, Jesus, Jesus, Jesus. Thank you, Jesus. Help me, Lord. I need your help, Lord. Tell him what you want, tell him what you need. Jesus listens to your prayers. He may not come when you call him, but he's always on time. Jesus, I'm in trouble. I need you. Come, Lord. Come, Lord Jesus. I love you, Lord Jesus. Jesus, I love you. Jesus, I'll never forget you, Jesus."

Rev. John Mark began to sing over the whole church. "I'm a solider in the army of the Lord / I'm a solider in the army of the Lord." The whole church began to sing, so beautiful to see and feel the spirit of God.

Rev. John Mark came home late that night after church.

My wife lying asleep in bed, and I'm standing here looking at her. I never told her about the fifteen years of my life left. I didn't want to put her through the pain. I've preached about how I was saved from a life of sin. But in my heart, I knew the Lord would take care of Mary. I love her so much, and I'm standing here thinking many thoughts to myself. But I can't worry about the end because I have a job to do for my Lord Jesus.

Rev. John Mark read a little of the Bible before he got ready for bed:

> Because he has set his love upon me, therefore, will I deliver him. I will set him on high because he has known my name. O love the Lord all ye saints, for the Lord preserveth the faithful and rewarded the proud doer. I will love thee, O Lord, my strength. The Lord is my rock and my fortress, and my deliverer, my God, my strength, in whom I will trust, my buckler, and the horn of my salvation, and my high tower. My soul has kept thy testimonies, and I love them exceedingly. Thou shall love the Lord thy God with all thy heart, and with all thy soul, and with all thy mind.

> The Lord is my shepherd, I shall not want. He maketh of me to lie down in green pastures, he leadeth me beside the still waters. He restoreth my soul, he leadeth me in the path of righteousness for his. (Psalm 23)

John began to sing, "I must see Jesus / I must see Jesus for myself." Many came and gave their life to God with tears in their eyes. Rev. John Mark said, "God so loved the world that he gave his only begotten son Jesus, that who so ever believe on him will never die."

The saints of God began to sing, "I must see Jesus / I must see Jesus for myself." Many was baptized and filled with Holy Spirit that night. The Lord mercy endureth forever.

After that night, there were so many calls asking Rev. John Mark to come and pray for their love ones, also can Rev. John Mark come to their church, and calls from faraway. Rev. John Mark couldn't fill the calls he got, but he filled as many requests as one man can do.

There was a message left at the church where Rev. John's home church. The woman was asking if Rev. John Mark would pray for her sixteen-year-old daughter who was in a mental hospital. The young woman was back at home with her mother in a few weeks. It was the mother's faith and love for her daughter that made thee whole.

That night at church, Rev. John Mark asked the members of the church, "How deep is your faith? How deep is your faith? Amen. Jesus said, 'But without faith it impossible to please him, for he that cometh God must believe that he is, and that is a rewarder of them that diligently seek him. By faith, Moses was hid for three months by his parents because they saw that he was proper child. By faith, the walls fell down after they were compassed about seven days.' Amen. How deep is your faith in God? Amen. 'By faith, Sara herself received strength to conceive, seed, and give birth to a child. Also by faith, Moses passed through the Red Seas by dryland, which the Egyptians assaying to do were drowned.' Amen. 'By faith, Noah, being warned of God of things not seen as yet moved with fear, prepared an ark to the saving of his house by which he condemned the world and became heir of the righteousness which is by faith.' Hallelujah. Hallelujah. Thank you, Jesus. Have faith in God. Amen. With this faith, I can. Hallelujah, Hallelujah. Amen. Jesus said, 'Thou whosoever say unto this mountain, be thou removed, and be thou cast into sea, and shall not doubt in his heart, but shall believe that those things which he saidth shall come to passed, he shall have whosoever be saidth.'"

Rev. John Mark talking to the saints of God, "Tum with me to St. Luke chapter 8 verse 47. And when the woman saw that she was not hid, she came trembling and falling down before him, she declared unto him before all the for what cause she had touched him, and how she was healed immediately. Amen. And Jesus said unto her, 'Daughter be of good comfort, thy faith hath made thee whole. Go in peace.' Hallelujah. Thank you, Jesus. How deep is your faith? Hallelujah. How deep is your faith? God shall wipe away all tears from your eyes. Amen. Amen. If I can just touch him, my Lord, my Lord. Keep your trust in God at all times. Hallelujah. Hallelujah. Amen."

Rev. John Mark in closing the service for the night, "Let God touch you, let him put a new song in your heart."

Rev. John Mark visited a woman in a hospital, who had one of her kidneys removed, and she wanted prayers. "O give thanks to the Lord, for he is good and mercy endureth forever. Lord remember David, and all his afflictions. Have mercy upon me, O God, according to thy loving kindness, according unto the multitude of thy tender mercies blot out any transgression. Have mercy upon me, O Lord, consider my troubles which I suffer of them that hate me, thou that liftest me up from the gates of death. Help me, O Lord, my God. O save me according to thy mercy. Have mercy upon me, O Lord, for I am in trouble. My eyes is consumed with grief, yea, my soul and my belly. I cried unto thee, save me, and I shall keep thy testimonies. Praise ye the Lord, for his mercy endureth for ever. Praise ye the Lord. Amen."

Rev. John Mark was asked to visit a Baptist church. "It was the house of the Lord. Tonight, I want you to believe that with God all things are possible. With men, this is impossible, but with God all things are possible. Amen. Thank you, Jesus. Jesus said, 'Behold I have told you before. That no man takes my life. I have the power to lay it down of myself, and the power to take it up again.' Amen. Amen. Thank you, Jesus. Thank you, Jesus. And God shall wipe away all thou tears from their eyes, and there shall be no more death, neither sorrow, nor crying, neither shall there be any more pain, for the former things are passed away. Amen. And I heard a great voice from heaven saying, 'Behold, the tabernacle of God is with them. And he will dwell with them. And they shall be his people. And God himself shall be with them, and be their God. For thou art great and doesn't wondrous things, thou art God at alone.' Amen.

"All things are possible with God. Believe today, saints of God, that God hath spoken once, twice have I heard this that the power belong unto God. What shall we say to these things? If God be for us, who can be against us? And the God of peace shall bruise Satan under your feet shortly. The grace of our Lord Jesus Christ be with you. Amen. Amen.

"Nor height, nor depth, nor any other creature, shall be able to separate us from the love of God, which is in Christ Jesus, our Lord. Amen. Amen. Jesus said, 'If thou can't believe, all things are possible to him that believe. Hallelujah. Hallelujah. Amen. Amen. But to us, there is one God, the Father of all things, and we believe in him. And one Lord, Lord Jesus Christ, by whom are all things are possible with him. Amen. Whom God bath raised having loosed the pains of death because it was not possible that he should be hold of it. Amen.

"For David speaketh concerning him, I foresaw the Lord always before my face, for he is on my right hand that I should not be moved. Amen. Because thou will not leave my soul in hell, neither will thou holy one to see corruption. Amen. Amen. For with God, all things are possible. Hallelujah."

Rev. John Mark traveled from church to church, preaching the Gospel of Jesus Christ. "Let the church say amen, amen! We bless you in the name of Jesus, our Lord. Bless is everyone that fear the Lord that walketh in his ways. Behold that thus shall this man be blessed that fear the Lord Jesus. Amen. For the Lord commanded the blessing even life forever more. The Lord will give strength unto his people. The Lord will bless his people with peace. Amen. For the Lord will bless the righteous with favor with thou compass him as with a shield. Hallelujah. Hallelujah. I cried unto the Lord with my voice, and he heard me out of his holy hill. Amen. Amen. Bless the Lord, O my soul, all that is with me. Bless his holy name, Jesus, and forget not his benefits. Amen. Amen. Bless ye the Lord, all ye his hosts, ye ministers of his that do his pleasure. Amen. Amen. Blessed be the Lord, for he hath showed me his marvelous kindness in a strong city. Amen. And blessed be the Lord God, the God of Israel, who only doeth wondrous things. Hallelujah. The whole earth be filled with his glory. Amen and amen.

"Jesus said, 'I say unto you, love your enemies, bless them that curse you, do good to them that hate you, and pray for them which despitefully use you, and persecute you. Hallelujah. Thank you, Jesus. Amen.' Let the whole church bless his holy name, and all thy works shall praise thee, O Lord, and thy saints shall bless thee. Amen. Amen."

Rev. John Mark came home that night after a blessed sermon.

"'Lord make me to know mine end, and the measure of my days, what it is, that I may know how frail I am (Psalm 3:1).' Lord, how are they increased that trouble me! Many are they that rise up against me. Many there be which say of my soul. There is no help for him in God. Amen. But thou, O Lord, art a shield for me, my glory, and the lifer up of mine head. I cried unto the Lord with my voice, and he heard me out of his holy hill. Amen. I laid me down and slept. I awaked, for the Lord sustained me. I will not be afraid of ten thousands of people that have set themselves against me round about. Arise, O Lord. Save me, O my God, for thou have smitten all mine enemies upon the cheekbone, thou have broken the teeth of the ungodly. Salvation belongeth unto the Lord, thy blessing is upon thy people. Amen. Amen. Psalm 95:6 says, 'O come, let us worship and bow down. Let us kneel be the Lord our marker.'

"Surely his salvation is nigh them that fear me of the Lord. But I have trusted in thy mercy. My heart shall recipe in thy salvation. The Lord is my light and salvation, whom shall I fear? The Lord is the strength of my life of whom shall I be afraid? But the salvation of the righteous is of the Lord, he is their strength in the time of trouble. Help us, O God, of our salvation, for the glory of thy name and deliver us, and purge away our sins, for thy name sake. 'Let the whole church say amen, amen! And cried with a loud voice saying, 'Salvation to our God which sits upon a throne. And that, knowing the time, that now it is high time to awake out of sleep, for now is our salvation nearer than when we believed. Amen. And take the helmet of salvation, and the sword of the Spirit, which is the word of God. Amen. But let us, who are of the day, be sober, putting on the breastplate of faith and love, and for a helmet, the hope of salvation. Amen. Amen.

"The spirit of the Lord God is upon me because the Lord hath anointed me to preach good tidings unto the meek. He hath sent me to bind up the brokenhearted, to proclaimed liberty to the captives, and the opening of the prison to them that are bound. Amen. Let the church give our Lord his praise. Hallelujah. Thank you, Jesus. Amen.

"Praise ye the lord, praise ye the Lord servants of God. For his merciful kindness is greatness toward us, I will praise the Lord with my whole heart. Praise his glory is above the earth and heaven praise his name Jesus. Jesus said, 'Come unto me all ye that labor and ate heavy laden, and I will give you rest.'

"Let not your heart be trouble because my Lord is with you until the end. Amen. Tonight, saints of God turn with me to the book of St Luke 16: 'There was a certain rich man, which was clothed in purple and fine linen, and fared sumptuously every day. And there was a certain beggar named Lazarus, which was laid at his gate, full of sores. And desiring to be fed with the crumbs which fell from the rich man table. And it came to pass that the beggar died and was carried by the angels into Abraham's bosom. The rich man also died and was buried. And in hell the rich man lifted up his eyes and saw Lazarus in Abraham's bosom. And the rich man cried out in torment have mercy on me that I may dip the tip of his finger in water and cool my tongue, for I tormented day and night in this flame. Amen. Amen.

"Let the whole church bow our head in pray, giving all praise to our Lord Jesus Christ. The Lord is good, and his mercy endureth forever. Let the saints of God say out loud, 'His mercy endureth forever. Amen!

"O give thanks unto the our God for his mercy endureth forever. Be merciful unto me, O Lord, for I cry unto thee daily. Amen. Surely goodness and mercy shall follow me all the days of my life, and I will dwell in the house of the Lord forever. Amen."

Rev. John Mark preached at a church on the far east side of town. That night he talked about temptation and the lust after the flesh to unsaved the child of God. But God wants everyone to know about his goodness and mercy that's what you pray to our Lord and Savior, Jesus Christ. Blessed is the man that endureth temptation, for when he is tried, he shall receive the crown of life, which the Lord hath promised to them that love Jesus Christ. Amen. Amen. But every man is tempted when he is drawn away of his own lust and enticed. Then when lust hath conceived, it bringeth forth sin. And sin, when it is finished, bringeth forth death. The Lord knoweth how to deliver the godly out of temptations and to reserve the unjust unto the day of judgment to be punished.

"And my temptation, which was in my flesh ye despised not, nor rejected, but received me as an angel of God, even as Christ Jesus. Amen. Let the church pray to our Lord and Savior Jesus Christ. And lead us not into temptation but deliver us from evil, for thine is the kingdom, and the power, and the glory, forever and ever, more. Amen. Amen."

Rev. John Mark said, "'Let us saints of God say amen, amen, hallelujah! Tonight, I want you to glorify our God in prayers.' All the saints that fears the Lord, praise him. All ye the seed of Jacob, glorify him, and fear him, all ye the seed of Israel. All nations whom thou hast made shall come and worship before thee, O Lord, and shall glorify thy name. I will praise thee, O Lord, my God, with all my heart, and I will glorify thy name for evermore.

"Lord God of my salvation, I have cried day and night before thee. The Lord is gracious, and full of compassion, slow to anger and of great mercy. Be merciful unto me, O Lord, for I cry unto thee daily. That I may with one mind and one mouth to glorify God, even the Father of our Lord Jesus Christ. Amen. Amen. I have glorified thee on the earth. I have finished the work which thou gavest me to do. And now, O Father, glorify thine own self with the glory which I had with thee before the world was. Amen. And said unto me, thou art my servant. O Israel, in whom I will be glorified. Amen.

"Let the church say amen, amen! Behold my servant whom I have chosen, my beloved, in whom my soul is well pleased. I will put my spirit upon him. And he shall show judgment to the Gentiles. Bless is that servant that low thou Lord Jesus Christ. Servant of God and the Lord shall help thee and deliver thee. He shall deliver thee from the wicked and save thee because he trusts in him. Make thy face to shine upon thy servant save me for thy mercies sake.

"Let them curse but bless thee. When they arise, let them be ashamed but let thy servant rejoice. Amen. Praise the Lord, praise, O ye servants of the Lord, praise the name of the Lord. Amen. The Lord redeemeth the soul of his servants, and none of them that trust in him shall be desolate. I am thy servant give me understanding that I may know thy testimonies. Amen. Amen.

"Servants of God are blessed with holy oil. In God have I put my trust. Amen. Amen. Save me, O Lord, according to your love in kindness and mercy. My soul waits for thou only upon God, for my expectation is from him. My soul thirsteth for God, for the living God. When shall I come and appear before God? Amen. O keep my soul and deliver me. Let me not be ashamed, for I put my trust in thee because thou will not leave my soul in hell with thou suffer thine holy one to see corruption.

"Return unto thy rest, O my soul for the Lord has dealt bountifully with thee. For thou have delivered my soul from death, mines eyes from falling. I will walk before the Lord in the land of the living. Amen. Amen. My soul waits for the Lord more than they that watch for morning. I say more than they that watch for morning. Amen. Amen. Bless the Lord at all times. Bless the Lord, O my soul. Bless the Lord, O my soul and forget not all his benefits. Bless the Lord, O my soul, and all that is within me, bless his Holy name. Amen.

"Lord, gather not my soul and all that is within me. Bless his Holy name. Amen. Lord gather not my soul with sinners, nor my life with bloody man. Lord show me thy ways, O Lord, teach me thy paths. Let the whole church say amen, amen! Praise ye the Lord, for he is good and his mercy endureth forever. Sing unto the Lord a new song, and his praise in the congregation go his saints. Amen. Amen. Let everything that have breath praise the Lord."

Rev. John Mark traveled to Cleveland to preach at small church.

"Amen. Saints of God, if a man dies, can he live again? Job asked God that question. If a man dies, can he live again? All the days of my appointed Tim will I wait, till my change come. Thou shall call, and I will answer thee. Thou well have a desire to the work of thine hands. For now, thou numberest my steps. Dost thou not watch over my sin. And whosever liveth and believeth in me shall never die yet shall live. Amen. Amen.

"But thanks be to God, which giveth us the victory through our Lord Jesus Christ. Therefore, my beloved brother, be ye steadfast, unmovable, always abounding in the work of the Lord. Amen.

Rev. John Mark a messenger of our Lord Jesus Christ traveled from church to church preaching the Gospel of Jesus Christ. "For God is not unrighteous to get your work and labor of love, which ye have showed toward his name, in that ye have ministered to the saints and do minister. Amen. Amen. Look upon mine affliction and pain and forgive all my sins. For thou Lord art is good and ready to forgive and plenteous in mercy unto all them that call upon thee. Rejoice in the Lord, ye righteous and give thanks at the remembrance of his holiness. O come let us worship and bow down. Let us kneel before the Lord our marker. O worship the Lord in the beauty of holiness, kneel before him all the earth. Amen.

"All the earth shall worship thee and shall sing unto thee. They shall sing to thy name. Amen. I will worship toward thy holy temple and praise thy name for they are loving kindness and thy truth. For thou has magnified thy word above all thy name. But as for me, I will come into thy house in the multitude of thy mercy, and in thy fear will I worship toward thy holy temple. Amen.

"The Lord our God worship at his holy hill, for the Lord our God is holy. Exalt ye the Lord our God and worship at his footstool, for he is holy. Amen. O come worship him all ye saints of God. All the ends of the world shall remember and turn unto the Lord. And all the kindreds of the nations shall worship before thee. 'Praise ye the Lord. O give thanks unto the Lord, for he is good, for his mercy endureth forever. I will praise thee with my whole heart before the Gods will sing praise unto thee Lord. Amen. O give unto the Lord, for he is good because his mercy endureth forever. Amen.

"I love the Lord because he has heard my voice and my supplications. O Lord, thou has searched me and known me. O Lord search me, O God, and know my heart, try me, and know my thoughts. Amen. The Lord looked from heaven. He beholdeth all the sons of men. Be merciful unto me, O Lord, for I cry unto thee daily. O Lord give ear unto me, pray and attend to the voice of my supplication. With my whole heart have I sought thee, O let not wander from thy commandments Amen.

"Let thy tender mercies come unto me that I may live, for thy law is my delight. In thee, O Lord, do I put my trust. Let me never be ashamed, deliver me in thy righteousness. O Lord, salvation belongeth unto thee, Lord, thy blessing is upon thy people. Amen. Know that the Lord is God. It is he that has made us, and not we ourselves. We are his people and the sheep of his pasture. Cast thou upon the, and he shall sustain thee, be shaft never suffer the righteous to be moved. Amen. Amen.

"Lord, truly my soul waiteth upon God, for him come my salvation. I cried with my whole heart, hear me, O Lord, I will keep thy status. The righteous thou O Lord, and upright are thy judgments. Righteousness of thy testimonies is everlasting, give me understanding, and I shall live O Lord. Amen. It not easy to live a righteous life, but I thank God through Jesus Christ our Lord and Savior. So then with the mind, I myself serve the law of God. But with flesh, the law of sin. Thank you, Jesus. Amen. Amen.

"Saints of God tum to Psalm 51. Have mercy upon me, O God, according to thy loving kindness, according to the multitude of thy tender mercies blot out my transgressions. Wash me thoroughly from my sin, for I acknowledge my trans and my sin is ever before me. Amen. Against thee, thee only, have I sinned and done this evil in thy sight, that thou mightiest be justified when thou speak. Behold, I was shape in iniquity and in sin did my mother conceive me. O Lord, hide thy face from my sins and blot out all mine iniquities. Amen. Create in me a clean heart, O God, and renew a right spirit within me.

"Cast me not away from thy presence and take not thy holy spirit from me, O Lord. Lord, restore unto me the joy of thy salvation and uphold me with thy free spirit. Amen. O Lord, open thou my lips, and my mouth shall show forth thy praise. Thy sacrifices of God are a broken spirit, a broken and a contrite heart, O God. I will praise thee among the people. I will sing unto thee among nations,

O God. Amen. Amen. In the house of God, O God, I will seek thy good. Amen.

"In my distress, I called upon the Lord and cried unto my God. He heard my voice out of his temple and my cry came before him, even into his ear. Preserve me, O God, for in thee do I put my trust. O Lord, preserve my soul, for I am holy. O thou my God, save thy servant that trust in thee. O Lord of my salvation, I have cried day and night before thee. Truly my soul waiteth upon God. Amen.

"O Lord, my soul longeth for thee, my heart and my flesh cried out for the living God. My God, my God, why has thou forsaken me? Why art so far from helping me and from the words of my help me. Help me, O Lord. O my God, I cry in the daytime, but thou hearest not, and in the night and am not silent. O Lord, I am poured out like water, and all my bones are out of joint. My heart is like wax, it is melted in the midst of my bowels. O God, hear my cry, O Lord, attend unto my prayer. Amen."

Rev. John Mark said, "He that dwells in the secret place of most high shall abide under the shadow of the almighty. I will say of the Lord, he is my God, in him will I trust. O Lord, I will say of the Lord, he is my refuge and my fortress, my God. In him, will I trust, O God. He shall cover thee with his feathers and under his wings shall thou trust. The truth shall be thy shield and buckler. Thou shall not be afraid for terror by night nor for the arrow that fly by day. O God, for the pestilence that walk in darkness nor for the destruction that wait at noonday, Amen.

"A thousand shall fall at thy side, and ten thousand at thy right hand. But it shall come not nigh thee. Amen. Amen. Because thou hast made the Lord, which is my refuge, even the most hithe habitation. For there shall no evil befall thee, neither shall any plague come nigh thy ling. O Lord, he shall give his angels charge over thee, to keep thee in all thy ways. Amen.

"Let the church say amen, amen, and give thanks to our Lord Jesus Christ, our savior. Let the saints of God say it out loud, 'I will bless my Lord at all times,' say it, say it. Amen. Hallelujah, Hallelujah. For my God has shown me loving kindness in the morning, and thy faithfulness every night. Amen."

Rev. John Mark visited the sick and prayed with for them. "The righteous cries, and the Lord hears and delivered them out of all their troubles. O love the Lord, all ye saints, for the Lord preserve the faithful and plentifully reward for the proud doer. Amen. Be of good courage, and he shall strengthen your heart, all that hope in the Lord. Amen. Amen. Let's Pray."

Rev. John Mark continued doing the Lord work until the end. "It is a good thing to give thanks unto the Lord and to sing praises unto thy name, O most high. For our hearts shall rejoice in the Lord because we have trusted in his holy name. Amen. Amen. O God is not unrighteous to let your work and labor of love, which you have shown toward his name, in that you have ministered to the saints of God. Amen. Amen. O come let us worship and bow down. let us kneel before the Lord our maker. O worship the Lord in the beauty of holiness, kneel before him all the earth. All the earth shall worship thee and shall sing unto thee, they shall sing to thy name. Amen. Worship, O Lord, all ye saints of God. Rejoice in the Lord in righteousness and give thanks at the remembrance of his holiness. I will worship toward thy holy temple and praise thy name for thy loving kindness is forever. Amen.

"But as for me, I will come into thy house of the Lord with thy multitude of tender mercy. And in thy fear, will I worship toward thy holy temple. Amen. The Lord is thy keeper, the Lord is thy shade upon thy right hand. I wilt praise thee with my whole heart because he has known my name. I love the Lord because he has heard my voice and my supplications because he has inclined his ear unto me, therefore, will I call upon him as long as I live. O Lord, truly I am thy servant, and the son of thine handmaid, thou has loosed my bonds. Amen. Amen. O give thanks unto the Lord, for he is good because his mercy endureth for ever.

"Let house of the Lord say that his mercy endureth forever. Let them know that fear the Lord say, that his mercy endureth forever. Amen. Amen. O Lord, I beseech thee, O Lord. O Lord, I beseech thee, send now prosperity. Blessed be he that come in the name of the Lord. We have blessed you out of the house of the Lord. O give thanks unto the Lord, for he is good, for his mercy endureth forever."

Rev. John Mark came home that afternoon and read from the book of Psalm. That night at church service, Rev. John Mark said, "God so love the world, that he gave his only begotten son Jesus, that whosoever believe in O Lord Jesus Christ shall never die. For God sent not his son into world to condemn the world, but that the world through him might be saved. God is a spirit, and that they worship him must worship him in spirit and in truth. Amen. Amen. O Lord, my God, how excellent is thy name in all the earth! Who has set thy glory above the heavens. O God, I will praise thee. O Lord with my whole heart, I will show forth all thy marvelous works. Thank you, Jesus. Thank you, Jesus. O Lord, our Lord, how excellent is thy name in all the earth. I will bless the Lord at all time, and his praise shall continually be in my mouth.

"I sought the Lord, and he heard me and delivered me from all my fears. Blessed be the Lord, for he has shown me his marvelous kindness in a strong city. O taste and see that the Lord is good. Blessed is the man that trusts in him. The Lord is my light and my salvation, whom shall I fear? The Lord is the strength of my life, of whom shall I be afraid? When the wicked, even my enemies and my foes, came upon me to eat up my flesh, they stumbled and fell.

For in time of trouble, he shall hide me in his pavilion. In the secret of his tabernacles, shall he hide, he shall set me up upon a rock. And now shall mine head be lifted up above my enemies round about me; therefore, will I offer in his tabernacle sacrifices of joy. I will sing. I will sing praises unto O Lord."

Rev. John Mark said, "Let the church say amen, amen. If it had not been for the Lord who was on my side. Now may saints of God say, 'If it had not been for the Lord who was on our side, when men rose up against us. Amen. Amen.' They that trust in the Lord shall be as Mount Zion, which cannot be moved, but abide forever. As the mountains are round about Jerusalem, so the Lord is round about people forever and ever. Do good, O Lord, unto those that be good, and to them that are upright in their hearts."

Psalm 121, "I will lift up my eyes unto the hills, for my help comes from the Lord, which made heaven and earth. He will not suffer thy foot to be moved. He that keeps thee will not slumber.

Behold, he that keeps Israel shall neither slumber nor sleep. The Lord is thy shade upon thy right hand. The Lord shall preserve thee from all evil. He shall preserve thy soul. The Lord shall preserve thy going out and thy coming in from this time forever and forever more. Amen. I was glad when they said unto me, let us go into the house of the Lord. Because of the house of the Lord our God, I will seek thy goodness and mercy. Amen. Amen.

"With my whole heart, have I sought thee, O let me not wander from thy commandments. Thy word have I hid in mine heart, that I might not sin against thee, O Lord. I will meditate in thy and have respect unto thy ways. O Lord, I will delight myself in thy statutes. I will not forget thy words. O Lord, I will praise thee with upright-ness of heart when I learned thy righteous judgment. I will keep thy statues. O forsake me not, O Lord. I will sing of the Lord. O Lord, I will bless thy name forever and ever. Every day will I bless thee, and I will praise thy name forever and ever. Great is the Lord, and greatly to be praise, and his greatness is unsearchable. The Lord is gracious and full of compassion, slow to anger, and of great mercy. I will speak of the glorious of thy majesty, and of thy wondrous works. They shall abundantly utter the memory of thy great goodness and shall sing of thy righteousness. My mouth shall speak the praise of the Lord, and let all flesh bless his holy name forever and ever.

"Praise the Lord, praise the Lord, O my soul. O Lord, I will sing a new song unto thee. O God upon a psaltery and an instrument of ten strings, will I sing praises unto thee. O praise the Lord, sing unto the Lord. O Lord, save me. O God give ear to words of my mouth. For strangers are rising up against me, and oppressors seek after my soul. O Lord, they have not set God before them. Behold, God is mine helper. The Lord is with them that uphold my soul. He shall reward evil unto my enemies, cut them off in thy truth. I will freely sacrifice unto thee. I will praise thy name, O Lord, for it is good. For he has delivered me out of all my trouble, and my eyes have seen his desire upon my enemies. O come, let us sing unto the Lord. Let us make a joyful noise to the rock of our salvation. O sing unto the Lord, bless his name, show forth his salvation from day to day. O love the Lord, hate evil. He preserveth the souls of saints, he delivers them out of the hand of the wicked.

"For the Lord is good. His mercy is everlasting, and his truth forever. Who shall separate us from the love of Christ Jesus? Shall tribulation, or distress, or famine, or persecution, or nakedness, or peril, or sword? Lord, in all these things, we are more than conquerors through him that loved us. For I am persuaded that neither death nor life, nor angels, nor principalities, nor powers, nor things present, nor depth, nor things to come. Nor height nor depth, nor any other creature, shall be able to separate us from the love of God, which is in Christ Jesus our Lord. Amen.

"Yet he is not rooted in himself but endureth for a while, for when tribulation or persecution arise because of the worst by and by he is offered. Seeing it is a righteous thing with God to recompense tribulation to them that trouble you. And to you, who are troubled, rest with us when the Lord Jesus shall be revealed from heaven with his mighty angels. So that we ourselves glory in you in churches of God, fur your patience, and faith in all your persecutions and tribulations that you endure. Amen.

"For then shall be great tribulation such as was not since the beginning of time. Who comforts us in all our tribulation that we may be able to comfort them who are in any trouble. We ourselves are comforted by God. And not only so, but we glory in tribulations. Also knowing that tribulation work patience, and patience, experience and experience, hope, Amen. O Lord, that I may with one mind and one mouth. Glorify God, even the Father of our Lord Jesus Christ.

"By him, therefore, let us offer sacrifice of praise to God continually, that is the fruit of our lips, giving thanks to his name. I will greatly praise the Lord with my mouth. I will praise him among the multitude. O God, my heart is fixed. I will sing and give praise even with glory. I will praise the Lord with my whole heart. Lord, I have glorified thee on the earth. I have finished the work which thou gave me to do.

"And now, O Father, glorify thou me with thine own self with the glory, which I had with thee before the world. Amen. O Lord,

I will praise thee, my God, with all my heart. The grace of Lord Jesus Christ, and the love of God, and the Holy Ghost be with you. Amen. The Lord looked from heaven, he behold all the sons of men. Beloved.

"Now are we the sons of God? And it does not yet appear what we shall be, but we know that, when he shall appear, we shall be like him, for we shall see him as he is. Amen. Amen. Behold what manner of love the father has bestowed upon us that we should be called the sons of God. Therefore, the world know us not. God fulfill my joy that you be like mine having the same love, being of one, according to one mind.

"Finally, be of one mind, having compassion one to another, love as brother, be courteous. O Lord, let this mind be in you which was also in Christ Jesus. Grace be with you all, Amen. Thou will keep him in perfect peace whose mind is stayed on thee because he trusts in thee. For I, the Lord thy God will hold thy right hand, saying unto thou fear not, I will help thee. The holy one of Israel. O thou shall love the Lord thy God with all thy soul and with all thy mind. He shall cry unto me, thou art my Father, my God and the rock of my salvation. Bless our God and Father of our Lord Jesus Christ, which according to his abundant of mercy. For this is his covenant that I will make with the house of Israel, said the Lord. I will put my laws into their minds and write them in their hearts, and I will be to them a God, and they shall be to me a people. Grace be with you all, Amen. Grace be with all them that love our Lord Jesus Christ in sincerity. Amen. Amen.

"O salvation belong unto the Lord, thy blessing is upon thy people. Amen. Trust in the Lord forever, for in the Lord Jesus Christ is ever lasting strength. The grace of our Lord Jesus Christ be with your spirit. Amen. O Lord, I trust in the mercy of God forever and ever. But the day of Lord will come as a thief in the night, which the heavens shall pass away with a great noise, and the elements shall melt fervent heat. Amen. Amen.

"O let us, therefore, come boldly unto the throne of grace that he may obtain mercy and find grace to help in time of need. Help, Lord, for the godly man cease for the faithful fall from among the children of men. They speak vanity, everyone with his neighbor with flattering lips and a double heart do they speak. The Lord shall cut off all flattering lips, and the tongue that speak proud things. But I trust in thee. O God be not fare from me. O my God make haste for my help. O God make haste to deliver me, make haste to help me, O Lord. O my God, I cry in the daytime, but thou hear not and in the night I'm not silent.

"My Lord have mercy upon me. Lord, be thou my help. But please, O Lord, deliver me, O Lord, make haste to help me. My soul waits for the Lord. He is our help and our shield. I will lift up my eyes unto the hills from whence come my help. My help comes from the Lord, which made heaven and earth. Behold, God is mine help. The Lord is with them that uphold my soul. God is our refuge and strength. A very present help in trouble. O help Lord, help Lord. My God, My God, why has thou forsaken me? Why art thou so far from helping me. Be not far from me, for trouble is near, for there is none to help. But I am poor and needy, yet the Lord thinks upon me, thou art my help and my deliver, O my God. O Let thy mercy, O Lord, be upon us, according as we hope in thee. Amen. But I trust in thee."

Rev. John Mark received a call at his home. Someone called for his help, a man was fighting his wife, it was a domestic violence. Rev. John Mark went over to the couple's house. Rev. John Mark was putting the woman in the car. At that time, the woman's husband came out of house with a gun. He began shooting at his wife, but the bullet hit Rev. John Mark in the back. At that moment, a great man of God was killed. On the day of the funeral and on the way to cemetery, Rev. John Mark was walking in the clouds with his Bible under his arm. Rev. John Mark walking home to glory, to his Lord and Savior Jesus Christ. Amen. Amen.

ABOUT THE AUTHOR

S helley Frinkley is a married homemaker and mother of five children: two daughters, three sons. What inspired her to write was the death of her youngest son, Ishmael. Ishmael was killed on the streets of Detroit nearly twenty years ago.